GRANGE-ENDERS

by

Maggie Walker

Illustrations by Chris Walker

FURTHER COPIES OF THIS BOOK ARE AVAILABLE FROM:

FutureLink Publishing
16 Harford Square, Chew Magna, Bristol BS40 8RA,
Tel: 01275 334145 Fax: 01275 331301
E-mail: publishing@futurelinksw.co.uk   www.futurelinkpublishing.co.uk

© FutureLink Publishing 2007

To Julie who changes children's lives

GRANGE-ENDERS

Contents

Episode 1:   Being new   1

Episode 2:   Dilemmas, dilemmas . . .   8

Episode 3:   Roller-coaster   14

Episode 4:   Dionne's diary   20

Episode 5:   Good day, bad day   25

Episode 6:   Now that's what I call
             teamwork. Not.   31

Episode 7:   The fight   40

Episode 8:   Sorting it   50

Episode 9   The challenge   57

Episode 10: Getting there   66

Episode 11: Result!   75

Episode 12: The final farewell   81

Episode 13: Then and now   89

Episode 1
Being new

Part 1: Eddie's story

EDDIE

I was so scared I would be late and now I'm way too early. The caretaker has just unlocked the tutor room with KF on the door, but I'm not going in - not until I've found the toilets. It's the thing that's been terrifying me most about this new school, the nightmare stories I've heard about what the older kids do to the new ones in the toilets; so I'll go while it's empty. It's the fifth time I've had to go since I woke up. Mum tried to make me eat another breakfast; she said I must have lost the first one a few times over.

The other thing I have to do before I see anyone is scrape some mud onto my shoes. My granddad polished them like a mirror for me; I didn't tell him they were embarrassing - I told him they were great.

1

I go into the empty tutor room and look around. It's really sad and bleak, needs pictures or posters or something to cheer it up.

The others slowly begin to arrive; most of them seem to know each other and start chatting and mucking about. I try to look normal but I feel like a right saddo sitting there on my own. Then I catch the eye of this girl. She looks OK so I try smiling, thinking I probably look like a complete loser.

Instead of just ignoring me, she comes over and sits down by me. I take a deep breath.

'Hi, I'm Eddie,' I say.

'Hi, Eddie, I'm Laura,' she says, and then before I know it, we're chatting, and suddenly it begins to feel OK. When some other kids join in with us I start to wonder what I'd got myself so worked up about.

After a while most of the kids are chatting, except this one sitting on a table behind me. I turn round to talk to him, but as I do, he puts his feet on my chair and his shoes get mud on my trousers.

He doesn't apologise or say anything, so I glare at him and then ignore him.

Then the door opens and this woman walks in, who I suppose is Miss Forest, our tutor. She is big and broad with this plaited hair close to her head and bright red lipstick. She is wearing this flowery dress and green high-heel shoes. She looks OK, smiling round at us, until the kid behind me says:

'Welcome to your tutor group, Miss K Forest,' in this really sarky voice. She stops smiling then and asks him his name.

'Rafiq Hassan,' he goes like he's some sort of celebrity. She doesn't look like she's impressed with Rafiq Hassan; she just tells us all to sit down. As we're all getting settled, this really fit girl rushes in through the door, and when the tutor says to her,

'You are?' she says,

'Late, I suppose.'

I have to admit it was funny, but when we all laugh, she looks ready to die of embarrassment. I would have felt the same. I hate being late and to have everyone laugh at you is gruesome. Dionne the girl's name is. She sits down behind me, and the tutor woman goes and has a word with her. She says she'll talk to her later.

Then it turns out that the woman isn't Miss Forest anyway, she's Mrs King, head of something or other and is only being our tutor because Miss Forest is ill. So we still don't know what our real tutor is like.

Your first job,' says Mrs King, 'is to get to know each other. Choose someone you don't already know and ask them to tell you three interesting things about themselves. Be prepared to tell the rest of the group one of those interesting things. You have ten minutes.' And she sits down at her desk and just watches.

I would like to ask that Dionne, but I don't have the nerve, and Laura grabs me anyway, so I stick with her. In the end, Dionne goes over to this lonely looking girl and partners her. I knew she'd turn out to be gorgeous inside as well as outside, but she'd never look at me; not in a hundred million years.

The kid, Rafiq, who put mud on my trousers is left without a partner but he doesn't seem bothered. Maybe that's what he wanted. He looks like the sort of kid who gets what he wants. I wish I did.

Part 2: Rafiq's story

RAFIQ

I sit on a table at the back of the room swinging my legs. It's nothing like the classroom in our primary school. It's small and stuffy, and there's nothing on the walls except peeling paint. Grim. I don't know any of the kids in the room, except Rosie Brown who was in my class at my old school, but she's not someone I'd ever speak to. She's not exactly smart - we used to say if she was any dumber you'd have to water her. She's sitting on her own, biting her nails and chewing her lip. She looks scared. I watch the other girls trying to pretend they're not scared; joking around, touching their hair. The boys are chatting to each other, not to me, but that doesn't bother me. I put my feet up on the chair in front of me. This kid gives me a look, but I don't move them.

There's no way I'm scared of anything at this new school. I know all about it. My brother, Prahlad, is in year 10, and he's told me everything I need to know. He says the teachers think he's great because he's so smart. He told me that Miss K. Forest, our tutor, is new, only just trained as a teacher. 'You'll be able to do just what you want,' he told me. What I want is to be what I was at my old school: the smartest kid in the year - in every way. I look around and think there's not much competition.

Just as I'm thinking this, Miss K Forest walks into the room. It goes totally quiet. Everyone stares. She looks around at the kids one by one. No one moves. I lean back on the top of the table. When her look lands on me, I go,

'Welcome to your tutor group, Miss K Forest.'

'You are?' she says. I tell her.

'Good morning, Rafiq Hassan,' she says. 'Please sit on your chair.' The other kids begin to snigger. They're so lame.

'Good morning, tutor group KF,' she says. 'Please all sit down on your chairs.'

We clatter into the seats, moving bags onto the floor and coats to the back of chairs. Suddenly the door bangs open and this girl storms in. Miss K Forest looks at her,

'You are?' she says.

'Late, I suppose,' says the girl, tossing her head. The class erupts, laughing. The girl shoves her way through the bags and sits down in the space next to me.

'I meant, what is your name?' says Miss K Forest and her voice is low and quiet, like a growl. The laughing stops. The girl stares at her.

'Dionne Taylor,' she says.

The class watches Miss K Forest. She walks past the bags to the back of the room where I'm sitting. She goes right up to Dionne.

'Come and see me later, Dionne,' she says, really quiet. I know Dionne's going to get it.

Then Miss K Forest turns to the rest of us.

'I am Mrs King, head of lower school,' she says. 'Miss Forest is unwell so I will be your tutor until she returns.' Nobody speaks. So she isn't the new tutor. I thought she looked old.

She asks us to do something with a partner and then she plonks herself down behind her desk. For a few minutes it is chaos, kids rushing round trying to find someone to work with. I just sit back up on the table, looking around to see who I want to do this with. Others pair up, until I see

everyone has a partner except Rosie Brown, Dionne and me. Rosie looks like she might cry. I realise I'm going to have to work with a girl, and am just about to ask Dionne, when she goes over to Rosie.

'OK to work with me?' she says.

'Triffic,' says Rosie, looking stupidly happy for the first time. Doesn't she know Dionne only chose her because she was the last girl left?

Episode 2
Dilemmas, dilemmas ...
Eddie's embarrassment

Part 1

EDDIE

Lunchtime and I can't believe there are nearly three hundred kids in this canteen. It's so noisy I can't hear myself think. I get my lunch, but I can't see anyone I know, so I find a space on a table with about six kids I've never seen before. They move over to make room for me.

I soon find out that one of them, Karl, is a real joker. Before I've even started eating, he has the whole table in stitches. It feels good, having a laugh, like I'm really beginning to fit in. Then that Rafiq kid comes over with his tray of food. When Karl sees him, he says,

'Spread out your stuff, all of you,' so we all stick out our elbows and move ourselves to fill up the spaces on the table. Rafiq just stands there, until a dinner lady sends him to the next table.

Then Karl says something about Rafiq, something disgusting and racist. The other kids burst out laughing.

Karl is looking at me to see if I'm laughing too, and it seems like, for a split second, the whole room is frozen. I know I have to make a decision. I look over at Rafiq.

Part 2

I'm not sure if he's heard what Karl has said, but I know that if I go along with it, it will be as bad as if I'd said it myself. I also know that if I don't go along with it, I'll look like a loser, and they'll probably start on me too.

I ask myself what difference will it make what I do? I tell myself Rafiq deliberately got mud on my trousers. Everyone on the table seems to be looking at me, all six of them. I feel my stomach churn, but it doesn't stop me. I do this big, fake laugh - joining in with them. And feel awful.

Rosie's risk

Part 1

ROSIE

I am on the field, kicking a ball around with these girls I've met, Katie and Suzy and some others. We leave our bags on the side. When it's nearly time to go in, we collect our bags, but one of them doesn't belong to any of us. Suzy picks it up, 'I'll see who's it is,' she says, and starts to look inside. We all gather round. She pulls out some books with the name, *Laura Macdonald* on them. I remember Laura is in my tutor group, but before I say anything, Suzy pulls out this scabby dirty little stuffed dog.

'Yuk,' she screams, dropping it on the mud, 'it's gross.' The others laugh. Suzy looks in the bag again and pulls out a pink book.

'Hey, see what we've got here,' she giggles, 'Laura Macdonald's diary.'

She looks round at us,

'Shall I read it to you?' she asks. The others giggle too, and gather closer, Katie puts her arm through mine. Suzy opens the diary.

This is horrible. I don't want to be here. If that was my bag and my diary, I'd die of shame. I look at the stuffed dog lying on the ground. I can't help thinking I've got my Eeyore key-ring in my bag, just for luck. I expect Laura did the same. I know what Suzy is doing is bad and I don't want to be part of it, but Katie has hold of me, and if I say anything, the others will think I'm really sad. But I know how it feels to have your stuff messed with.

Part 2

I pull my arm away from Katie's. My heart is pounding and I feel myself going red, but I take a deep breath and shout at Suzy,

'Why don't you just leave her stuff alone?'

Suzy looks at me and says something I won't repeat. She throws the diary on the ground and marches off. Katie pushes me out of the way and runs after her.

I pick Laura's things up and put them back in the bag. As the bell goes I see Laura running over.

'Did I leave my bag here?' she says.

Dionne's dilemma

Part 1

DIONNE

My cousin, Dwayne, is in year nine and he's waiting for me, with some of his mates when I come out of school. The year nines don't start back until tomorrow. I stroll along with Dwayne and his gang; they're quality. I can see the other kids watching us and it feels great. Dwayne doesn't usually let me hang around with him - my grandmother doesn't let me hang around with him either, but I tell myself she won't mind me just walking home with him. We take up a lot of the pavement. People move out of the way as we go past. I feel kind of powerful. When we're passing the supermarket, Dwayne and his mate Ben, grab two trolleys from the stack.

'I think we'll have a little ride,' goes Ben.

'Splendid idea old chap,' laughs Dwayne.

The others are cracking up with laughter as they climb into the trolleys. Dwayne and Ben start pushing them along. I wish they wouldn't do that. I think what my gran would say. Suddenly, I don't want to be there; I don't want people to look at me, I don't want them to see me.

'Come on, Dionne,' yells Dwayne. 'Get in.'

I wish I could just run home. I don't feel powerful anymore, I feel s c a r e d, a n d wrong, but I don't want Dwayne and the others to think I'm a loser. I know he'll never let me hang around with him again if I don't join in. Two of the girls are already in Dwayne's trolley.

'Come on, Dionne,' they scream.

Part 2

I find myself climbing over the side and the girls pulling me in, laughing. I pretend to laugh too, but I feel more like crying. Dwayne begins to push us really fast. I feel sick. I wish I was anywhere else. I hear a man from the supermarket calling to Dwayne to stop. Dwayne laughs. The man runs after us. Dwayne is still laughing but he lets go of the trolley. The two girls jump out while it's going along. They run off. When I look round I can't see any of them any more. The trolley bashes into the fence and comes to a stop. My knees hit hard against the metal. I sit there waiting for the supermarket man who is coming over, looking, like, totally furious.

Episode 3
Roller coaster

Part 1

ROSIE

We're playing football before school. I dash forward, dribbling the ball, slip it past Katie, leg it down the left wing and curve it right over to Maddie. Maddie scores.

'Go Maddie. Go Maddie.' The girls in our team are cheering like mad.

'That was a fantastic goal,' I say to Maddie.

'That was a fantastic pass,' she says to me. We have a football hug. Then this older girl comes over.

'What's your name?' she says, looking at me.

'Rosie Brown,' I say, wondering what sort of trouble I'm in.

'Well, Rosie, we're trying out for the girls' under fifteens tomorrow lunchtime,' she says, 'I'm the captain. I think we could use you. Come along and have a go.' I can't believe it; the under fifteens want to try me out. I can't stop smiling.

'Wow,' says Maddie, and she's smiling too. Then Katie goes,

'They probably want you to play in goal, Rosie, you'd just have to stand there and no one could get the ball past you.' Everyone laughs, even Maddie.

I don't feel like laughing. I feel my face burning. I feel as if I've been hit hard in the stomach. Now I know everyone thinks I'm fat. I want the ground to open up and swallow me. I grab my bag and coat and leave them to it.

'Oh, she's sulking now,' Katie calls after me. 'Can't take a joke, then, Rosie?'

I stop for a moment. I think I'm going to hit her. Instead I take a deep breath and carry on walking.

First lesson maths. I'm still feeling bad. I can't think about anything except how fat and ugly I am and how no one likes me. I look over at Dionne and I think, she isn't fat, she's skinny and cool; everyone likes her. I am thinking so hard about how much I want to be like Dionne, and how much I don't want to be me, that I don't hear a word of what Mr Smith is saying as he takes us through the work.

'Right then,' he says, 'you all know what to do, so go ahead and do it.' The others begin to write. I look at him blankly.

'What is your name?' he says, sighing.

'Rosie Brown.'

'And what are you supposed to be doing, Rosie Brown.'

'Dunno,' I say.

'Well, if you'd been listening you would know,' he shouts, pulling at his hair, 'and if you think I'm going to tell you all over again you're wrong. You have thirty minutes to finish.'

I wouldn't have thought it was possible to feel worse than I did, but I do. Now I don't just feel fat and unpopular, I feel like a right thicko as well. I hate myself; I hate the teacher; I hate them all. I want to run out of the lesson. Eddie is sitting next to me. He pushes his book towards me, and whispers,

'Look, this is what you have to do.' He shows me how he's worked out the first problem from the board. It's actually quite easy.

'Do you get it?' he says.

'I think so.' He smiles at me.

'Thanks,' I go. Then Mr Smith comes over.

'Do you know what you're doing now?' he asks. He even sounds quite kind. I nod.

'Well, come and see me if you get stuck – but how about listening next time, Rosie Brown, eh?'

Part 2

In the canteen at lunchtime, the girls are talking about the new outfits they've bought for the year seven disco. I just hope no one will ask me what I'm wearing. My dad's just lost his job and new clothes are out of the question.

'What are you wearing Rosie?' asks Maddie.

'Haven't decided,' I mutter.

'My dad's buying me new shoes and everything, when he gets back,' Maddie goes on.

'He's away just now driving his lorry. What does your dad do, Rosie?' I shrug wishing she'd just shut up.

'He doesn't do anything. He got sacked,' I say, hoping that will shut her up. It does. She looks embarrassed and turns away to talk to Katie. I reckon I couldn't feel more crap if I was sitting by myself in the middle of a field in a rainstorm.

Dionne walks past us. The girls all call to her,

'Over here, Dionne, over here.' Dionne looks round, hesitating, then it's like she sees me and decides to sit down, right next to me. I'm amazed. She smiles at me.

'Hi, Rosie,' she says, ignoring the others. 'How's stuff? I've heard you're being tried for the under fifteens; that's so cool.' I feel like the sun is beginning to shine again. I smile right back at her. The others are all watching, listening.

'Who told you?' I ask her.

'Letitia, the captain, she's my cousin,' she says. 'I asked her if I could try, but she said I'd have to practise a lot more. She said you're pretty sound.'

'I'm not that good.' I feel myself blush.

'Well she thinks you are. You're so lucky, Rosie. I'd die to be as good as you and get in that team.'

I can't believe it. Me, Rosie Brown: a fat, stupid loser, and Dionne thinks I'm lucky. I think for a moment. I am almost too embarrassed to say what I want to say with everyone staring at me, but I do.

'Would you…would you like to train with me?' I say. I know I sound awkward and shy but I keep going. 'I go training most nights after school. If I get in the team I could try and help you get in too - if you'd like.'

There is silence on the table. The others are all waiting to see what Dionne will say.

She smiles.

'Lush,' she says, 'that would be great, thanks Rosie.' I feel like I've won the lottery.

Episode 4
Dionne's diary

DIONNE

8.45pm. It's exactly eleven weeks today since Mum and Chantelle went to London and I haven't even seen them once in that whole time.

I miss them so much, especially Chantelle. It's like there's this big gap where she used to be. Gran's OK but she's so strict and she's not exactly a laugh a minute. It's never fun like it was when we were all here, and since I got in trouble from the supermarket man I've been grounded. It's so not fair: Mum would never have grounded me.

20

At first when they went away it was fine. Mum phoned me all the time and Chantelle sent me presents like this really cool bag. But tonight I've phoned her five times and she's just not answering. She told me to phone her whenever I need to, but how is that any good if she's never going to even answer?

It's so lonely now; even Gran's hardly ever here. Tonight she's off at her dancing or some church thing. She's always away doing the teas or dishing out soup to the old people or something. She said I could go with her as long as I kept out of trouble, but I didn't want to, so Minger Mo from next door had to come and 'baby sit' me. Baby sit! I'm twelve years old. And anyway I know Mo only comes round so she can stuff her face with Gran's cooking.

If only there was something to do round here it wouldn't be so bad – and Rosie agrees with me. We'd love to have somewhere we could meet up in the evenings that Gran didn't freak out about not being safe. But we know that's not going to happen. The only thing anyone ever does for young people round here is moan. No one cares about us. Oh, why couldn't Mum have taken me to London as well as Chantelle? She's only five years older than me. Mum says they'll come back when they've made a bit of money but I keep thinking it might be years. I can't bear it; I'm sometimes so afraid I'll never see them again.

Chantelle was my best friend in the world as well as my sister. How could she just go off and leave me? I am so unhappy. It's like there's a piece of me missing. I sometimes close my eyes and pretend she's here and think of all the things I'd tell her like I always used to tell her everything. But then when I open my eyes I remember she's miles and miles away so what's the point?

9.30pm. I just went downstairs to get a drink and Minger Mo is sat in Gran's chair, watching TV with this great plateful of chicken and rice she's helped herself to.

'You alright, Dionne?' she goes to me with her mouth full. Gross. I just nodded.

I can't bear this. Why can't things stay the same? Well, I don't care if Chantelle has gone off and left me. I don't care at all. I hate her. And she probably hates me as well or she wouldn't have gone - and she'd answer her phone. I am so miserable.

9.45pm. Rosie's just phoned to tell me she's been picked to play in the team on Saturday and I'm going to be sub. Fantastic. This training is beginning to pay off and I've only done it for a week. But I have to say it's like totally tough. I didn't realise till I started how not fit I am – three times round the pitch and I'm ready to drop and then the trainer hollers at me to get some speed up.

'Are you serious about this, Dionne?' she yells, so I nod and try to go faster.

But Rosie is so cool. She never gives up. I would never have stuck it every night if she hadn't kept me to it.

It's funny really, like training is such hard work and I'm exhausted most of the time, but when I'm doing it I forget about Chantelle and Mum and how lonely and miserable I am. It all seems worse when I sit here on my own.

Rosie's feeling bad too at the moment, but with her it's because of her dad. I never see my dad. I never even knew him, but hers has lost his job or something so they're totally broke. She says he just sits around being miserable all day. He used to be a good laugh – going with her to training, watching her play and taking all of them out to Alton Towers and stuff. Now she says it's like he's so fed up he hardly even talks to her. I suppose it gets her down the same as it gets me down when Chantelle doesn't answer her phone.

I'll just try her one more time. Maybe she's working. If she's not there I'll leave a message and tell her I'm sub on Saturday. She'll be well pleased. She says if I get to play in that team she's coming down to watch. I can't wait.

10.15pm. Gran's home at last. She's just told me she's taking me up to London to see Mum and Chantelle on Sunday. I'm soooo happy. I'll just have some of that lovely chicken and rice before I go to bed.

Episode 5
Good day, bad day

Part 1

EDDIE   I've been here a while now and things are settling down. I'm still sort of mates with Laura, but I've started hanging around with Karl as well. Karl doesn't rate Laura, he says she's boring.

Anyway, it's last lesson, English. We're supposed to be writing a letter someone would be proud to receive. I'm writing to my dad. I haven't seen him since I started this school and I know he'll be well pleased when he gets it, but I've only got as far as my address because Dionne is sitting in front of me and I'm trying to see the phone number she's written on her letter. I've got the first four numbers and I'm feeling good, only seven more to go. I know I'll never have the guts to phone her, but it'll be good to know I could.

Dear Dad, This new school is alright, I write, when I realise I can just make out Dionne's next three numbers. I write them down next to the others – wicked, only four to go. I go back to my letter. *I've made some*… then Dionne moves her arm a bit and I get the whole number. Cool!

Well, it's cool until I realise it's the end of the lesson. I can't believe it. I've only written about five lines. The teacher comes round looking at what we've done.

'You think that letter will make your father proud, Eddie?' she says.

After school Laura is waiting for me at the bus stop. I told her I'd get the bus with her because she hates it on her own, but Karl and his mates are there so I pretend I haven't seen her and go over to them. When I sneak a look to see if Laura's seen me, she's staring at me like I've hit her or something. She gets on the bus by herself. Karl laughs.

'Result!,' he says, 'I don't know why you hang around with her, Eddie. Tell you what, let's walk, then we can spend the bus fare.' I know I should get home quickly because I promised to help my granddad on his allotment, but I say,

'OK, cool.'

Part 2

Almost every person we pass on the street, Karl makes a joke about until we are falling about laughing. Then we see this woman coming towards us. She is wearing these weird clothes and a man's hat and she walks funny. Karl starts walking like her – exactly like her - until we are laughing so much we can hardly stand up.

But, then I see the woman's face. She looks gutted. She looks like she wants to crawl under the hedge and hide. She looks afraid. Suddenly I don't feel like laughing. I feel crap.

'Where have you been?' my mother says, the minute I walk through the door.

'Your granddad waited ages for you, and now he's at the allotment by himself. You know he's too old to do all that digging.'

'We had to stay behind to do some science,' I mutter, 'I forgot to tell you.' She stares hard at me but she doesn't say anything.

When Granddad comes home, Mum says to him, 'Eddie had to do some extra work at school.'

'Good lad, Eddie,' he says, smiling at me all kind of proud, 'it's important to work hard.'

After tea I go to my bedroom. Well it's not just mine, it's Sam's too, my little brother. I want to be by myself, but the minute I lie down on my bed to think things over, he starts hassling me. I wish he'd go and watch Eastenders.

'Play *Tony Hawks* with me Eddie?' he begs. I don't want to play some stupid skating game; I don't want to do anything, but I look at his face, all hopeful, and I think, it's not his fault I feel so bad; so I say,

'Fine then, but watch out because I'm going to beat you.' He laughs, all happy. Then he beats me.

Part 3

'You're really good, Sam,' I say to him, 'wicked.' He can't stop smiling.

'Thanks Eddie,' he says, 'that was great.' Later when Sam is asleep, I sit at the table thinking things over. I look at Dionne's phone number for a while, wishing I had the guts to phone her and knowing I never will. Then I get a piece of paper from my bag, chew my pen for a bit, then start to write: *Dear Dad, This new school is* OK. *I've made some good mates. I miss you a lot and I'm looking forward to seeing you soon.* I write loads. I take care with the writing. I even use a dictionary. I think, what would Dad like me to write? It takes me nearly an hour. I read it through and picture his face reading it. I put it in an envelope. I'll get a stamp and post it tomorrow.

I hear granddad coming upstairs, puffing and panting. He doesn't put his head round the door to say, 'Night Eddie, lad,' like he usually does. I hear him in the bathroom, coughing. I hear the TV downstairs and know Mum is down there watching it. I start to feel bad again, like my heart has sunk into my stomach.

I go downstairs. The TV is on but Mum isn't watching it; she's staring at nothing. I sit down next to her but I don't know what to say. Then I take a deep breath.

'Mum, I didn't do extra work after school,' I say, 'I walked home for a laugh.' She looks at me for a moment and I can't tell if she's happy or sad. Then all she says is,

'I'm glad I've got my real Eddie back. There was a fake version here earlier.' She ruffles my hair.

'You get to bed now, young man, I want to watch the news.'

I hear granddad getting into bed. I can't tell if it's the bed creaking or his bones. I put my head round his door.

29

'Hello, Eddie, lad,' he says, 'not asleep yet?' I sit on his bed. He's wearing stripy pyjamas and smells like Granddad: soap and tobacco and old man.

'I'm sorry I didn't help you at the allotment today, granddad,' I say, 'I'll come tomorrow, promise.'

'You come when you can,' he says, 'You've got your own life now.'

We sit there quiet for a while, then he says, 'You're a good lad, Eddie, one of the best.' I can't take this. I shake my head.

'I'm not,' I tell him. He grips my hand with his. His is covered with big brown freckles and his nails are yellow.

'Listen here, Eddie,' he says to me, 'I've known you all your life and I say you're a good lad, because I know it.'

And I look at him but I can't speak because suddenly it feels like something's stuck in my throat.

Episode 6
Now that's what I call teamwork. Not!

Part 1

All ninety of us from year seven are on camp. The minute we pile off the buses this camp-leader bloke starts yelling about how we've only got fifteen minutes to unpack our stuff before we meet on the field.

'And I hope you're all wearing old clothes and you've remembered to leave your mobile phones behind,' he goes. Karl smirks 'yeah right'. He chucks his bag down on the bed next to mine and we follow the others to the field.

It's all very well saying we've got fifteen minutes but I've got this really bad stomach ache and I have to go to the loo and I'm last in the queue. When I come out every single person has gone and I've got no idea where the field even is.

The field is enormous and covered with little piles of stuff like wooden poles and string and plastic sheeting and tools. Karl laughs and picks up a piece of wood from one of the piles, getting ready to chuck it.

'You there - put that down,' yells the camp leader. Karl scowls then hurls the wood back down on the pile, muttering under his breath. When the camp leader looks away, he

gets out his phone and starts texting.

'Sit down on the grass, all of you,' hollers the camp leader. I look round to see what group Dionne's in, but I can't see her anywhere.

DIONNE

The camp leader says to get in groups of five then he tells us what we've got to do, but I'm looking round to see where Rosie is and whose group I want to join and not listening properly. I see Eddie, I don't mind working with him. He comes over with this Karl who is messing about with his phone. That's three of us.

I hate working in groups and anyway everyone else seems to have found a team already. I stand there feeling like a dork until this woman in a red t-shirt comes over.

RAFIQ

'I'm one of the helpers,' she says, 'there's a group of three over there, go and join them.' I look over and see Dionne, but she's with that smug Eddie and Karl who I can't stand. I'm thinking there's no way I'm working with those two when the woman says,

'Go on. Don't hang about. You're wasting time.' So I have to go. But I go slow.

ROSIE

When I eventually find the field I see all these kids doing stuff in groups. I don't have a clue where to go or what to do.

'You're late,' says this bloke in a red t-shirt, 'go and work with that group over there.'

It's Dionne's group he's pointing at which is great until I see Rafiq is with them as well and my stomach-ache suddenly gets worse. He's looking at me as if I'm an idiot – the way he always looks at me.

'Ignore him, Rosie,' says Dionne, as I go over, 'what are we supposed to be doing anyway?'

'I Dunno,' I say, 'I only just got here.'

'Well, whatever it is, it'll be a waste of time,' says this Karl kid.

I know what to do but I don't bother telling them. Why should I? I'm just pulling out some wood and plastic sheeting from the pile to make my own shelter when loser Eddie starts.

RAFIQ

'Get lost, Rafiq,' he goes, 'you can't do that – it's for all of us. We're supposed to build a shelter together.'

'Oh leave him to it, Eddie,' says Karl, 'There's no way I'd work with him anyway – in

34

fact, if he's in the group, you can count me out.' He flops down on the grass with his back to us, and starts playing something on his phone.

'I wouldn't work with him either,' I say to myself.

DIONNE If we're supposed to build a shelter together then I'm not going to let Rafiq take all the stuff. I go over and grab some poles. Rosie follows me and picks up some string.

'Don't bother, Rosie,' says Rafiq, 'the guy forgot to mention that you need a brain before you can start.' Rosie's face goes bright red and I don't know if she's going to hit him or cry. She chucks the string on the floor and storms off. I'm just about to go after her when one of the helpers goes over. He stops her and says something to her quietly. I can see her calming down but when he brings her back she's still red.

'Take no notice of him,' I tell her, 'it's him that's got no brain.'

Part 2

EDDIE

The helper stands there looking round at us.

'You don't seem to have got very far,' he says. 'Perhaps you should work out some sort of plan together before you go any further – then decide what each of you is going to do.' He spots Karl.

'You there' he calls, 'this isn't optional. Come and work with your team.'

Karl rolls his eyes. 'Boring,' he mutters as he gets to his feet and shoves his phone in his pocket.

'And I'll look after that for you,' says the helper, holding out his hand. Karl looks like thunder as he hands over his phone. The helper turns back to the rest of us.

'I suggest you get going,' he says, 'half your time has gone already.'

ROSIE

Dionne and Eddie try to work out some sort of plan.

'Come on Rosie,' Dionne calls to me, 'you're good at this sort of stuff, so what's the best way to put these poles up?'

'Triangles,' I say. I go over and help her fix some poles together with string, but my stomach hurts and I wish I was home in bed.

When we've got the frame done, Eddie gets Karl to help him put some plastic sheeting over.

'As long as I don't have to work with him,' mutters Karl glaring at Rafiq; but Rafiq isn't listening. He's just carrying on building his own shelter. Typical.

RAFIQ

The camp leader blows a whistle and tells us to sit down. I look round. There are seventeen completed shelters, all different shapes and sizes, there's my little one, and then there's the one Eddie and that lot built. It's a disaster, only half finished with the cover falling off. I laugh, thinking I made the right decision when I started my own. Mine looks OK - just big enough for me.

DIONNE

The camp leader and the helpers walk round. They discuss each shelter with each group and work out what score they should get. The score is partly for how good the shelter is and partly for how well the group worked together. One group gets nineteen out of twenty. I'm so dreading what they'll say when they get to us. Eddie and Rosie stare down at the floor but Rafiq has this pleased-with-himself look as he sits next to the stupid, tiny shelter that he made with all the best stuff. The team leader asks some questions. I tell him the triangle frame was Rosie's idea. Rosie tells him that Eddie and me tried to get us all to work together. Eddie says we all know we wasted too much time and didn't plan it properly. Karl says nothing.

The camp leader has a chat with the helpers.

'We've decided to give you a score of seven,' he says at last, 'because you seem to have learned some valuable lessons.'

Then he turns to Rafiq.

'What is this?' he says to me.

'It's my shelter,' I tell him, 'the group was rubbish so I worked on my own.'

'I see,' he says. He's quiet for a minute looking round at the helpers then he turns back to me.

'You get zero,' he says, 'because you didn't do the task. If your group had had five people

38

instead of four, and if they'd had all the equipment, don't you think they might have done better?' I can't even answer him. I have never in my life got zero for anything, but he hasn't finished.

'I want your group to talk over what went wrong,' he says, 'and what you might have done differently.' Then he walks away. That Karl stands there sniggering and I am so mad I don't care who knows about it.

'I can tell you what went wrong,' I yell, 'it was you, stupid Rosie Brown, arriving late - and it was the rest of you not even listening. None of you idiots knew what to do except me.' Before anyone speaks the team leader has turned around and come back. I don't know what he's staring at me for.

'I want you each to think about your own contribution,' he says, 'it's sometimes easier to blame someone else than to consider what you did, or did not, do.' The others look at each other then they look at me. I stare back thinking they're all totally stupid.

'Remember the only person you can change is yourself,' says the camp leader, walking away again. Well, he can say what he likes, they can all say what they like but I've got nothing to say. Nothing. None of this is my fault.

Episode 7
The fight

Part 1

Monday

We've got to do some project thing that's supposed to have something to offer the whole of year seven. Rosie and I talked about it over the weekend but we can't think what to do. I'd like to get some sort of dance thing going, maybe sponsored or something, but she says not enough would join in. We're still thinking.

For the first time in my whole life, my granddad doesn't get out of bed. He looks ill. He looks old. He tried to say 'Morning Eddie, lad,' but his voice was all raspy and horrible. Mum says she's going to get the doctor. We're supposed to be thinking about this year seven project thing, but all I can think about is him.

EDDIE

RAFIQ

I've had enough of saddo Eddie. He is seriously getting on my nerves. I know the best way to get to him though. At break time I go over to where Dionne's standing with Rosie and some of the other girls. I see Eddie hanging around close by as usual.

'Hi, Dionne,' I go, 'd'you mind if I ask you something?' She gives me this frozen look but I'm not bothered.

'I've got an idea for this Y7 project thing that might just work,' I say, 'I thought we could set up our own website and I thought you might like to work with me on it.'

'Cool,' go a couple of the girls. 'We could cover like fashion and music.' Dionne doesn't say anything, but I can tell she's interested.

'Don't bother, Dionne,' says Rosie, 'why would you want to work with him?'

'Well, there's no harm in listening,' says Dionne. She turns back to me. 'Why me, anyway?' she says.

'Why not?' I say. 'You're a good writer and you know what's cool; It's got to have stuff for girls and people rate you. I thought you might be interested. Think about it.'

I smile at Eddie as I wander off. He looks completely wound up. LoL.

Tuesday

EDDIE

Rafiq's been trying to chat Dionne up, get her to do some stupid website with him, but I know she won't. She can't stand him. Anyway, I've got other things on my mind.

When I got home from school last night, Granddad was up and sitting in his chair. He said he wanted to walk to the paper-shop and get some air. Mum said, 'No way, you know what the doctor said,' but Granddad wasn't having it.

'Eddie will go with me,' he said, 'I'll be alright. Don't start treating me like an old man.'

It's only round the corner but it took us forty minutes to walk to the shop and back. Granddad had to keep stopping and he couldn't breathe properly. By the time we got back, his face was a weird colour and he was leaning on me so hard I didn't know if I could hold him up. Mum took one look at him, laid him on the sofa and called an ambulance. Now he's in hospital – intensive care.

Dionne's going to do this website with me. I knew she would in the end. Now I can really wind Eddie up and that stupid Rosie Brown.

RAFIQ

Wednesday

EDDIE

Mum says Granddad isn't too good. He's out of intensive care but he's got to stay in hospital. This morning I had to take my sister and brother to school so Mum could go and see him before work. That almost makes me late. I hate being late. Then I see Dionne and Rafiq going into class together, chatting like they're some sort of item. I can't believe this.

I see Eddie coming and I lean really close to Dionne. We're only talking about the website, but I can see it's getting to him. It's wicked. I arrange to meet Dionne later so we can work on the design.

RAFIQ

At break I see her talking to Eddie. I go over, butt right in and start talking about the website with her. Eddie stands around looking like he's about to go psycho. When we go back into school, I lean up to him and smile.

'Dionne's well fit,' I go. 'I wouldn't mind…' He takes a step towards me but this kid, Karl, pulls him back.

'Don't get your hands dirty,' he says. Karl is the sort of racist scum I'd expect Eddie to hang around with.

EDDIE

I try to keep my mind on my work but half of it is on my granddad and the other half is on Rafiq and Dionne. What does she see in that self-centred idiot? He'd better leave her alone.

School's over and there are loads of kids by the buses. I see Eddie with Dionne. I go over.

RAFIQ

'Hi Dionne,' I say, 'I've been thinking - my brother's got this media programme. I was wondering if we should look it over. It's got brilliant graphics.' I can see Eddie's totally listening.

'OK, sounds alright.' says Dionne.

'Well, d'you wanna come round mine.' I look round at Eddie and give him this wink, but he grabs hold of my arm.

'Hey, steady,' I go, but he doesn't move. He grips on to me really hard. 'Back off, Rafiq,' he says, practically spitting in my face, 'just leave her alone.'

Part 2

This is going too fast for me. I was only trying to wind him up. I don't do fights. He is pushing me in the chest and Dionne starts yelling,

RAFIQ

'Don't be stupid, Eddie. Eddie leave him.' Before I can even think what to do, all the kids around are going, 'fight, fight, fight.' They gather in this circle around us. I hold up my hands and move backwards, trying to laugh it off, but he's still coming after me.

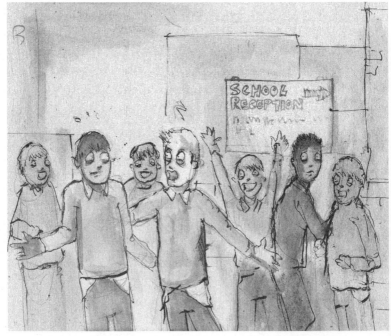

I catch a glimpse of my brother running towards the school. I see that Karl. He calls out the usual racist stuff

from the back of the crowd where he knows I can't get him. I feel my temper rising.

'Just leave Dionne alone,' Eddie is shouting now, 'you think you're all that, Mr Wonderful, but you're just a cocky frigging creep and if I see you near her again I'll...'

He lifts his fist but before he can touch me something flies right close to my face, but misses me and hits him hard on the head by his eye. It looks like a can of drink. It splatters all over him and bounces to the ground. I'm in total shock and pick up the can.

Eddie stands there holding his head and staring at me like he wants to kill me. Like *I* was the one who insulted *him*. Like it was me who threw the can. His face is suddenly dead white and I can see this blood pouring down. I wish I was anywhere else. Especially when I see the head striding towards us – he doesn't look happy......

Part 3

An hour later

EDDIE

'He is total scum and I don't care who knows.' That's what I tell the police. I don't know who called the police but I am in the head's office with two of them; there's blood all over me and a bandage over my eye. I don't want to be here. I need to get home.

'Look, I have to get out of here,' I tell them, 'it was him that started this. He's been getting at me for ages. I didn't do anything and he hit me with this can.'

' – no, I didn't see him do it but who else would it have been?'

RAFIQ

I am so mad. Why do I have to be here in the head's office with two policemen? My dad will go mental at me and it wasn't even me that started it. I didn't do anything. They're not even listening to Prahlad – at least he's backing me up - but they are like, 'well, he would say that wouldn't he?'. They obviously don't know my brother. Anyway – he would hardly have run to get the head if I had started it would he? Idiots.

48

'No, I don't know who threw the can,' I tell them. 'It wasn't me. It almost hit me first. How would I know? I didn't do anything. He grabbed hold of me and he would have hit me if the can hadn't hit him first. He's the one you need to be questioning'.

At last they let me go, and it's all like 'You haven't heard the end of this young man' – it's so unfair. When I get out there's still loads of kids around, it'll be all round the school tomorrow. Apparently one kiddy saw Karl throw the can but won't grass him up. Pathetic - scared to mess with Karl like everyone else in this stupid school.

And they've even got it in for Prahlad for spoiling a good fight. What a mess.

Episode 8
Sorting It

Part 1

A week later

EDDIE   Rafiq and I have to go to Mrs King's office. There's a man there with her. He's got decent trainers on and a stud in his ear. He doesn't look like a teacher.

'This is Sean,' says Mrs King.

I sit as far from Rafiq as possible.

'I've called you two here to tell you this has gone far enough,' says Mrs King. 'It's a week since that disgraceful fight and the atmosphere between you two is unsettling the whole tutor group. It has got to be sorted and Sean is here to help.'

'Try telling him that, not me,' mutters Rafiq. I turn away from him and fold my arms. The cut on my eye still hurts.

'We've had the police involved, and your parents,' says Mrs King, 'and we have to make sure it never happens again. Only you two can do that.'

I don't need reminding about parents being involved. 'How could you, Eddie?' my mother said to me about a million times over. 'Don't you think I have enough to worry about? What would your grandfather think?' I tried to tell her that none of this was my fault but she wasn't listening.

Rafiq has that stupid smug look on his face.

'This has nothing to do with me,' he says. 'I didn't do anything.'

Sean stands up. He is tall, about six foot four. He smiles. I don't smile back, nor does Rafiq. I don't want to be in here.

'OK, ready?' says Sean. 'Make sure you keep up.'

And he walks so fast out of the door and down the corridor we nearly lose him. He walks out on to the playing field then breaks into a slow jog. What is going on? He turns round.

'Stay close,' he calls, in a voice I don't feel like ignoring. He gains speed. We race after him.

Five minutes later Sean stops on the other side of the playing field. He is hardly out of breath but I am panting and Rafiq is holding his side.

'OK,' says Sean. 'This is what we're going to do.'

Part 2

Next day

RAFIQ

I can't believe we have to meet with this Sean bloke at lunch break every day; it's a nightmare. Not only do I have to listen to loser Eddie, I'm supposed to talk to him as well. What a waste of time.

Today we're meeting on the playing fields again. Sean makes us run there. He reckons it calms us down and then we have to do this slow breathing. I hate Eddie even more than before for getting me into this. I'm in major trouble with my father and it's all his fault.

Sean says it's time for us to explain what we're feeling. I roll my eyes. Eddie picks at the grass. Neither of us is saying anything.

'Before we start,' Sean continues, 'we have to agree that this time you will let each other talk without interrupting, OK?'

'Whatever,' says Eddie. I shrug.

'And try to talk about what you are feeling, not what you are accusing someone else of, alright?' I really don't want to do this. I know what I'm feeling - that Eddie is no one I want to be near.

'So who wants to start?' says Sean. I stare at the ground. We still don't speak. Then Sean says, 'Eddie?'

EDDIE

I don't even want to be here in school. I want to be at the hospital with my granddad. He's really ill. My mum spends half her life there so I have to keep getting breakfast and tea for Sam and Lucy. And now I've got to do this stupid thing with Rafiq so we can be best friends or something.

Sean asks me what I'm feeling. At first I don't answer him then I say,

'OK, I'll tell you what I'm feeling. I'm feeling that Rafiq is a…'

'Well you're a…' Rafiq shouts over me.

'OK, OK, hang on', says Sean. 'How you are feeling, Eddie, not what do you think of Rafiq'.

I pick at the grass until it's practically bald.

'Eddie?' Sean asks me again and I look up at him; and as I do my mind goes right away from that playing field to where my granddad is lying with a disgusting tube up his nose and a needle in his arm. And suddenly something cracks inside me and I can't really believe it but I'm telling him about what's on my mind - not Dionne, not Rafiq…. I'm telling him how worried I am about my granddad, and then I'm telling him something I can hardly bear to think about myself; I tell him my mum's told me he might die.

Nobody speaks for ages. I look over at Rafiq. He has his head in his hands.

RAFIQ

Eddie tells us about his grandfather nearly dying or something. It's horrible. When Sean asks me how I'm feeling what can I say? I can't stop thinking about when Prahlad got ill and I thought he was going to die. I think about the argument we had before he was taken off in the ambulance and how I'd told him that I hated him. I feel so bad – almost like - surely I'm not going to…?

Suddenly my voice gets all choked and I find myself admitting to Sean that right from the start I'd been trying to wind Eddie up; I'm telling him the whole Dionne thing was just a joke to get to him.

Sean sits quietly for a while then he asks Eddie what he thinks. He asks him if maybe he reacted so violently to what I was saying because he had all that other stuff on his mind. Eddie pulls at his shoelaces. Then he shrugs.

'Maybe,' he says. 'If I wasn't so – you know – maybe I could have ignored him.' We sit there a while longer. The bell goes for the end of break. Eddie stares over at the kids wandering back into school but I can tell he's not seeing anything.

'So,' says Sean, 'what happens now? We have to let Mrs King know you two can be in the same place without fighting or winding each other up. Can you?' I make myself look over at Eddie. Slowly he turns his head and looks back at me.

'Suppose,' I say.

'Yeh, suppose,' he says.

'Right then,' says Sean, 'sorted for now. See how it goes'. He climbs to his feet and begins jogging on the spot. Eddie and I walk back not looking at each other.

Later still

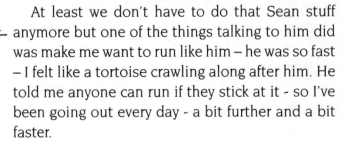

EDDIE

At least we don't have to do that Sean stuff anymore but one of the things talking to him did was make me want to run like him – he was so fast – I felt like a tortoise crawling along after him. He told me anyone can run if they stick at it - so I've been going out every day - a bit further and a bit faster.

Rafiq's been sort of OK. He's still doing the website with Dionne but I know now that's all it is. I know she'd never fancy him any more than she'd fancy me. She did ask me if I wanted to help with the design of the site and I told her I wouldn't mind. I haven't exactly thought about doing anything else for the project. When I asked her how Rafiq would feel about me being involved, she said he'd said it was OK. I know he's someone I'd never want to spend time with, but at least I don't want to thump him anymore. I feel a bit better anyway now Granddad's home.

RAFIQ

I only started that website idea to wind Eddie up and now it really seems to be happening. Dionne asked Eddie if he wanted to help with the design. I suppose that'll be alright. I won't need to have much to do with him. As long as Dionne doesn't get that brainless Rosie Brown involved, it should be alright.

Episode 9
The challenge

Part 1

ROSIE

We've got until the end of term to get this project planned, then the whole of next term to get it finished. I can't believe Dionne let that slimeball Rafiq sweet-talk her into working with him on his website. He only did it to wind Eddie up; but even after that stupid fight nothing I say will make her change her mind. She keeps saying he's not as bad as he was before the fight and I should just ignore him, but he's so up himself he's hard to ignore.

This website is a really good idea – even if it was Rafiq's. We've still got a lot of thinking to do but Eddie says he'll do the design - which is cool - and I reckon I can persuade Rosie to do a keep-fit page – she says she might as long as she doesn't have to talk to Rafiq.

DIONNE

EDDIE

Dionne, Rafiq and me get together to talk about this website. Rosie comes along with Dionne. The design ideas I've got go down alright, but when Dionne tells Rafiq that Rosie's going to do a keep-fit page, he says,

'You can't be serious - it was mostly her stupid fault the last thing we did was so crap. She hasn't got one idea in her pea brain. Why would I want to work with her again?'

At this point Dionne goes mental. She throws down all the stuff she's brought with her and starts yelling,

'I must have been off my head to think I could work with you, Rafiq. You know that wasn't Rosie's fault - it was as much yours as anyone's - and I'll tell you something else, if she's not in on this then neither am I.'

But Rosie's had enough. She stands up and grabs her bag.

'Oh, leave it Dionne,' she goes. 'I knew this wouldn't work if he was part of it and I was right. Count me out.'

So then Dionne stands up and grabs hold of her arm. 'Stay here, Rosie,' she goes, 'we're not doing it without you. If we do it without anyone, it's him. He may have thought of it in the first place but since then he hasn't had one single idea of his own, so all he can do is diss other people. He's just jealous.'

'Jealous?' says Rafiq, 'of her? Get real, Dionne.'

'Yes jealous,' yells Dionne, 'because you know she's better than you at everything. She's been picked for the football team because she's a brilliant player, she's fair, and she does what she says she's going to do. And she's had a million more ideas for this website than you. The only thing you've got is some keener of a brother in year ten. You're sad and pathetic Rafiq and everybody knows it except you.'

There isn't a sound. We all sit there with Rafiq looking at the floor and I don't know what to say. Then he reaches for his bag.

'Do it without me then,' he says really quiet, 'if that's what you want.' Nobody answers. He walks to the door. As he turns the handle I go,

'You leave now, Rafiq, and what Dionne said will be true. This may have been your idea but there's other people on board now. This is exactly what went wrong last time – we screwed up because we didn't try and work together. So why don't you come back - no stupid comments, no thinking you're too good for us, let's just do something that works out for once.'

Rafiq stands with his hand on the door handle. The room is so silent I can hear myself breathe. After a long, long moment he pushes his hair back from his face, takes a deep breath, comes back, and slouches down in his chair.

Part 2

A few days later

DIONNE

This is amazing; Rosie has planned this ace keep-fit page that shows how to measure your heart rate and what to do to get yourself really fit. I could have done with knowing all this before I nearly killed myself at training.

And there are loads of people involved now. There's a skating page, sports, music and all that sort of stuff. Maddie and Katie have planned this page called 'The Cringe Factor' - like when you fart just when it all goes quiet or walk round without knowing your skirt's stuck half way up your bum. They've got some great pictures. It's hilarious. And Laura and her mates are doing a page on how to be successful – they've got stories about different celebrities and all the stuff they had to do to make it big– they're putting together a 'top ten tips for success'. Laura asked Eddie to work out how to get music to go with it.

A few of us have planned a page with a quiz on how to know if someone fancies you. I'm going to try it out on Eddie; he's so cute. Even Rafiq has been OKish since I had a go at him about Rosie. He actually seems to be listening now.

Trouble with this website is everyone is doing all this cool stuff and I'm stuck with this totally boring keep-fit rubbish. Like who in year seven even cares about keeping fit except Dionne and me? But Dionne's really keen on me doing it and I can't let her down. Anyway, everyone reckons sport and keep-fit are the only things I know about.

Well, considering this was my idea in the first place I don't know if I should feel good that this website is getting so big, or really naffed off because at the moment I can't think of anything of mine that could go in it. Everyone else is involved. Maybe Dionne was right about me not having any ideas of my own. I just can't think what to do that anyone else would be interested in. I just don't like working with other kids. That's never been my thing. I'm a loner.

RAFIQ

I'm thinking I probably always will be a loner when this Li in our tutor shows me these amazing photographs he's taken of white tigers and rhinos at the zoo, and asks me if he can do a page about zoos being cruel. Li is totally geeky about animal rights, and at first I'm thinking, who cares anyway? But then I start to wonder about getting a sort of issues blog going - the sort of stuff that bugs people – not just animals but like racism or bullying; I could find out what people think, get them talking, bring it out into the open. Might be OK.

I've had loads of ideas for the design of this website and at first it was great – like I found 578 websites just for choosing the buttons - but now I see it's not something quick and easy or even fun. It's massive and it's totally hard work, and it's doing my head in trying to get it right. I've even had to cut down on the time I spend running – just when I was really getting into it.

I'm going to see the ICT teacher, Ms Wright after school today. It's a good job Granddad's home from hospital and doing OK. I could never concentrate if I had to worry about him as well.

Ms Wright showed me how to do loads of stuff then I spent half the night working on it at home. But today when I try to show her where I've got to, it turns out I didn't save it properly and I've lost every single thing – all those hours of work.

I am gutted; in fact I'm ready to jack the whole thing in and let someone else do it and good luck to them until Rosie says,

'Don't let that beat you, Eddie. We need you on this because you're brilliant – we'll help you, all of us, just tell us what to do. And think of all that time you put in – it would just be wasted if you chucked it in now.' She keeps on talking to me until I've calmed down, and when I think it over I know it makes sense. 'A quitter never wins and a winner never quits,' is what Granddad always says. In fact I'd be ashamed to go home and tell him I'd quit. So I agree to start again.

'Great – hey, Eddie, don't forget to hit the save button', says Rosie. Very funny. Not.

RAFIQ

My dad's really good with computers and he said he'd help Eddie with the design, so we're having a meeting round my house on Friday after school. First thing we've got to decide is what will go in the website and what won't. There's so many ideas flying around, we know we can't include them all, so we've told people that Dionne, Rosie, Eddie and I will make the decisions, as we were first to be involved; then we'll let them know.

Part 3

Friday:

ROSIE

I am mad as hell. What is the point? I spend hours and hours getting all this information on how to keep fit and reckon I'll just get it checked first by Mr Jenkins, the PE teacher, to make sure I've got the facts right; and does he say, 'How interesting, Rosie, that must have taken you forever?' Oh, no. He just glances over it, then hands it back to me with this sneery look and tells me I've made loads of spelling mistakes and I've got it all wrong about body temperature.

'If you want to make something public,' he says, looking down his nose at me, 'then get the science right and ....work with someone who can spell.'

I don't even bother telling him this is only the first draft. I don't bother telling him anything. I rip the whole thing up in front of him and dump it in the bin.

'Hmm, why not come back when you've grown up a little?' is all he says.

I have never felt so sick in my life. The others are right, I'm thick and stupid and I'll never be good at anything except football - and now we're having this meeting and I'll be the only one who hasn't done anything and it's all useless.

Episode 10
Getting there

Part 1

ROSIE

I go to where I said I'd meet Dionne to go to this meeting but she's not there. Maybe she's already gone. Well there's no way I'm going to Rafiq's on my own. I never wanted to go there anyway and now I've got nothing to show and I so don't want to tell Dionne I've let her down.

EDDIE

We said we'd meet by the buses but only Rosie is there looking totally fed up. When she sees me, she blurts out that she's not going to the meeting because Mr Jenkins told her the keep-fit page was rubbish and full of spelling mistakes. She says to tell Dionne she's sorry; then storms off.

66

I remember how she kept me going when I wanted to give up, so I go after her and tell her that the meeting is to talk about the whole of the website - not just the pages we've done and that we need her there because she's always fair and she's got good ideas about what people like. Then, when she's calmed down a bit, I tell her about how I've started running and ask her for ideas on how to get fit. She's starting to look a bit happier when Dionne turns up with Rafiq and his brother Prahlad.

DIONNE

Rosie looks like she's been crying but I don't want to say anything to her in front of Rafiq and Prahlad. Rafiq's dad is picking us up to take us to his, so we hang around until he comes. Rosie's really quiet the whole time.

ROSIE

Eddie's really, really kind. It's him who persuades me to come to the meeting. And he told me he's started running. I never knew he was into that stuff; he's quite cool sometimes.

When Dionne arrives she's with Rafiq and his brother so I don't get a chance to tell her about anything. Then Rafiq's dad arrives and drives us to their flat.

When we walk in I look around. It's totally massive but it's the messiest place I've ever seen. There are clothes and books and papers everywhere: on the floor, on the chairs – there's hardly even anywhere to sit. Rafiq's dad clears half of the table for us and warns us not to touch anything; then he goes off into this room, which Rafiq says is his office. I thought he was supposed to be helping us but he hardly says a word - not even to Rafiq or Prahlad, just tells Rafiq to keep the noise down because he's busy.

'He's always busy,' says Rafiq, and it's the first time I've ever seen him look embarrassed, 'He probably won't be able to help us after all.'

'So where's your mum?' Dionne asks him.

'She's in America at some conference,' he says, 'she's always busy too'.

By now I'm wishing I hadn't come; it's cold, I'm hungry, Rafiq looks like he's wishing we weren't there and Prahlad isn't exactly a bundle of laughs; but he soon disappears off somewhere to do his homework.

RAFIQ

We haven't been home five minutes before I start to think that meeting at mine is a really bad idea. My dad and Prahlad hardly speak to any of us; Dad's forgotten he's supposed to be helping us and hasn't done the shopping as usual, so there's nothing to drink, no biscuits, and everywhere is a total mess. I move my mum's boots from the middle of the floor and my dad's coat from one of the chairs and put them away.

Then I think we're here now so we might as well get on with it. So we sit at the space my dad's cleared on the table and go through all the ideas that people have given us and decide what we'll put in the website and what we'll leave out, including the stuff that us four have done.

My 'issues blog' idea goes down well, so that's going to stay. Then Dionne tells us about this quiz she's done with a few other girls to see if someone fancies you. It's quite a good laugh but when she tries out a few of the questions on Eddie, he just goes red and says, she should try it on a girl. Doesn't she already know he fancies her like hell? Anyway we reckon the quiz will make a good page so we vote to keep that in.

Eddie takes us through his designs, which are OK, but when Dionne asks about the keep-fit page, Rosie looks like she might cry. So then Eddie tells us that Mr Jenkins dissed Rosie's page because of the spelling and she'd chucked it. Dionne looks well fed up.

'That page was cool, Rosie,' she says, 'couldn't you do it again? I'll help.'

But instead of saying she'll do whatever Dionne wants like she usually does, Rosie just bursts out,

'No. I couldn't do it again, Dionne. I never even wanted to do it at all. I know you think it's good, but it's not what people are interested in – it's not even what I'm interested in. I only did it so I wouldn't let you down.'

DIONNE   I feel so bad when Rosie yells at me that she never wanted to do a keep-fit page, like I've been bullying her or something. I don't know what is going on with her. I mean she looked a bit weird when I tested out the fancying quiz on Eddie. What's that about?

So we all sit there kind of awkward for a few minutes, then Eddie asks her if there's anything she *would* like to do, and suddenly she's talking about getting a page going where she can get people interested in setting up a local teen-café with music and internet access and stuff. I sit there and stare at her, wondering where all this came from and where was I when she was figuring it out. Anyway, Eddie seems to think it's sound – in fact he says it's a brilliant idea - but the amazing thing is what Rafiq says. Instead of telling Rosie how hopeless she is and asking her why she's even bothering, he goes,

'Don't take this wrong, Rosie, but I could help you with the spelling if you want. I know I haven't exactly been the best team-player, but I am good at spelling and stuff, even if it is naff to admit it'. That's the first time I've ever heard Rafiq say he'd help anyone to do anything - and the first time he's admitted he's not brilliant at everything. And then, instead of sounding off at him, Rosie goes,

'Thanks Rafiq but I can spell alright if I'm interested. I think I just got careless with that keep-fit thing because I was bored.' Then she does this little smile at Eddie and he smiles back. What is going on?

Part 2

Two weeks later

ROSIE

It's been quite a couple of weeks. My dad took Dionne and me to see some local councillor about the town needing somewhere for teenagers to go and I told him my idea about setting up an internet café for young people. He seemed to think it was a really good idea and even said he'd talk to someone about possible premises. Then we went round some shops and businesses to see if they'd be interested in giving us funding. We're setting up a page on the website called, 'Somewhere to Chill'. It's going to be like a campaign blog where people can give their ideas about the teen café and get the whole thing moving. Dad's really into it. It's kind of got him going, so he's more like he used to be.

I've stopped moaning so much about my dad now I've been to Rafiq's house. I mean Rafiq's parents are so busy doing whatever it is they do, it's like they don't have any time for him at all. I even feel a bit sorry for him. Maybe he's the way he is because his home's so weird. Even when he was really down, my dad never shut himself away like that, and Mum says he's only low because of losing his job and not being able to buy us stuff – so I'm trying to understand him.

Dionne and I are getting on OK at the moment but it's not like it used to be, I wonder if it's because I told her I really like Eddie and I think he likes me. She did go sort of funny. Well she's never been bothered about him so what's her problem?

EDDIE

I've been working night and day on this website. I've had a lot of help from a lot of people and it's beginning to look good. We're calling it *Teen Power*. I've got most of the pages ready to go and on Friday after school we're going to see if it works. Rosie's been great, staying behind after school and all that. Dionne's been great as well, but if Rosie's with me, she kind of hangs back, almost like she wants me and Rosie to get together or something. No way; Rosie's nice but Dionne's the one for me.

DIONNE

Rosie told me she fancies Eddie and now she's started hanging around him the whole time but the trouble is that Rafiq told me Eddie fancies me. I feel so bad. I mean I like Eddie, I think he's great, but only as a mate and Rosie is my best friend and I don't want this to come between us. I don't know what to do.

I talked to Chantelle last night when she phoned me. 'Shall I tell Rosie she's wasting her time on Eddie?' I ask her, but Chantelle says if I do that, Rosie will think it's because I want him for myself. 'Just stay away from them both for a bit,' she says 'and let it sort itself out.' But I don't want to stay away from Rosie and I don't want her to get hurt or make a fool of herself and I can't stay away from Eddie because we're all involved in this website. Nightmare!

RAFIQ

It's six thirty on Friday night and we're all still in school, standing around in the computer room waiting to see if this *Teen Power* website will work. Half of year seven is here, Mrs King has just arrived with a few other teachers, and OMIGOD the head has just walked in.

Ms Wright helps Eddie sort the last few hitches. We all hold our breath. He hits the button, the music starts and – dah dah - there

it is, our very own website, live and kicking. I think we did it. RESPECT!

Episode 11
Result!

Part 1

RAFIQ

I can't believe this, we've got to go and talk to this panel of business people about how we designed the website and all that. There's some enterprise award or something and they're considering us for it. We're the only group out of year seven who've got to go to the panel and there's another group from year nine.

DIONNE

This time we are NOT going to screw up. We plan who's going to say what and this time everyone listens – even Rafiq – this one is just too mega to go wrong. Rafiq is so much better at the whole team thing these days but I think we've all

75

still got that nagging worry that he'll go back to being an idiot and ruin it for us.

And at the same time I'm trying to keep away from Eddie like Chantelle said.

EDDIE

Am I scared? This is the scariest thing I've ever done. Two men and three women in suits are sitting round this table. Mrs King is there as well; she introduces them, but after that she doesn't say anything. They've already seen the website working, we've done our presentation and now they ask us loads of questions.

It wouldn't be so bad if Dionne wasn't being so weird. She hardly ever even talks to me now and I have to tell these suits that we're working as a team.

Anyway I do it. I tell them how everyone got involved to help crack the technology problems; then Dionne and Rosie tell them about getting this amazing blog going to get funding for the teen café and how the whole community is getting on board, and Rafiq tells them about the issues blog, which he says has gone really big - dealing with all sorts of stuff like homophobia as well as racism and text bullying and stuff.

Then they ask us what we think you need to make a project work. They say they'd like to hear something from each of us. We look at each other and Dionne says I should start, so I say,

'You need a goal; you have to know what you want to achieve, like making it interesting to lots of different people in different ways, and getting it launched on time.'

Dionne says,

'You have to listen to each other and cooperate. We've all realised that it's tough sometimes not having it your own way – knowing that what you want isn't what everyone else would want.'

Then Rosie goes,

'You have to keep going even when you feel like throwing the whole thing in, even when people say things that you don't want to hear, like criticism. You have to know that mistakes can be what help you to do it better.'

Then the suits look over at Rafiq. At first he doesn't answer and I think he's going to blow it; Rosie is biting her nails, then he says,

'I think the most important thing you have to remember is that it isn't only about you; everyone can be involved in different ways, people are good at different things. You just have to find out what.'

They ask us a few more questions then they thank us and we leave.

Part 2

A few weeks later

It's the last day of term and we are in the hall with the rest of the lower school. The head is there and Mrs King, with a woman and a man. I recognise the man from that panel we talked to. The woman is young and skinny with a pierced nose. When we're all sat down, Mrs King introduces the woman. It's Miss K Forest, our actual tutor. She looks alright. She smiles over at us and says she's looking forward to being with us next term.

Then the man stands up and says he is going to announce the winners of that enterprise award we did our website for. He tells us loads of schools have been involved which is amazing. I had no idea it was so big - and we've actually got to the last six, so we've done really well. He says he's going to read out the list of prize-winners , and it's like the Oscars; he gets out this envelope and opens it and starts reading: 4th place, not us, 3rd place, not us, 2nd, not us, and then, I can't believe it, it's us: me, Dionne, Rafiq and Eddie. We've won the top award for our website!

I sit there totally stunned until I realise that Dionne is hugging me and yelling 'Omigod,' 'Omigod'. Then Eddie hugs Dionne. Even Rafiq is smiling. Everyone is clapping and cheering all around us. We have to go up on the stage and the man shakes our hands and congratulates us and tells us we've won a grant to help us develop the website further. I can't believe this. It's like the X-factor or something. I'm too dazed to have much idea about what is going on around us but I think it's all good. In fact when I'm back on planet earth I'll probably think it's the best thing ever.

Episode 12
The Final Farewell

Part 1

EDDIE

First day back after the holiday and it seems like almost everything is OK. It's really hot and sunny and after school Rosie says how about we go and get an ice-cream from the van. But Dionne just shrugs and says she's not bothered, and goes on home by herself. I'm standing there wondering what it is that's bugging her, when Rosie comes right out and asks me if I'll go out with her. I don't know what to say. I stand there for a minute like a complete wuss then mumble something like, 'You're really great, Rosie but I don't really want to go out with you because I still like Dionne'. Then I leg it.

But I can't stop thinking about it all the way home. At first I'm really mad at Rosie and thinking why did she have to go and spoil everything? But after a bit when I've calmed down I start feeling like a complete idiot. I mean, why did I have to tell her I liked Dionne? Why did I just run off like that? Duh! Funny thing is, by the time I'm close to home even thought I'm still embarrassed and all that, I can't help feeling a bit…well…somebody actually asked me out…me…hey!

I don't bother taking my key these days as Granddad's always in, but when I bang on our door there's no answer. I go round the back and I'm peering in through the window when Mrs Lepinski from next door yells to me that Sam and Lucy are with her and I need to go round there too.

'Where's Granddad then?' I ask her, climbing over the fence because it's quicker than going round.

'He's at the hospital, Eddie, with your mum,' she says, 'he got taken bad this afternoon. Your mum said you can all stay here until she gets back.' I feel my heart miss a beat. Mum told me if Granddad had another turn it would be dangerous. I start to panic and try to push past Mrs Lepinski to get to her phone but she holds onto my arm.

'I have to phone my mum,' I shout, trying to shake her off, 'I have to see if Granddad's OK'. Sam and Lucy must have heard me. They come and stand on Mrs Lepinski's step. They look frightened.

'See, I told you Eddie would be home soon,' Mrs Lepinski says.'You'll be alright now won't you?' Lucy runs over and grabs tight hold of my hand but Sam still looks worried.

'Look, there's some games in the cupboard in the kitchen,' Mrs Lepinski says, 'why don't you play something with your brother and sister, Eddie?' I open my mouth to tell her I don't want to play stupid games, I want to phone my mum and make sure Granddad's alright, but Lucy's dragging on my hand and Sam goes, 'Yeh, let's play Operation, Eddie,' with his face brightening up a bit. Then Mrs Lepinski looks really hard at me like she's trying to tell me something, so I shut my mouth and try to swallow down the panic and the fear and put on this big fake smile.

'OK, then, Operation it is,' I go.

Mrs Lepinski's made us about ten rounds of cheese on toast, we must have played every game in that cupboard and my face aches from trying to keep smiling when Mum comes home at last. I take one look at her and this icy fear grips my insides. Lucy grabs her round the legs and Sam buries his head in her jumper.

'How's Grand-dad?' I ask her, but it doesn't sound like my voice. She looks right back at me like she's holding onto herself, while she strokes Sam's hair, then Lucy's.

'He's not too good, Eddie, love,' she says, 'but let's get these little ones to bed and then I'll tell you all about it.'

Granddad's dead. That's what she tells me. He died that afternoon, soon after she got him to the hospital. But even when she tells me I don't believe it. I don't see how it can be true. Granddad can't die; he can't just suddenly not be there; the world can't just go on the same if he isn't in it anymore. I sit there for ages, kind of numb and cold then I go and sit in his room by myself until Mum comes looking for me and sends me to bed.

In the morning she tells Sam and Lucy. Lucy cries, but Sam just goes a bit white and bites his lip. None of us goes to school.

The next few days I walk around with this hollow feeling inside my stomach and this empty feeling in my life where Granddad used to be. Half the time I still don't really believe it and when I do believe it it's like I hate everything because I don't want it to be true. I don't want to go back to

84

school. I don't want to see anyone or speak to anyone, but after the funeral Mum says it'll help us if we all try and get back to normal. Normal? How can things ever be normal again?

Part 2

I walk in the tutor group and it seems like everyone stops talking. I don't care. I chuck my bag down and sit staring at the table. Nobody comes over; it's like they're all ignoring me. Well, great. I don't want anything to do with them anyway.

It carries on like that in all the lessons till lunchtime, then, when the bell goes everyone leaves except Rosie. She comes over. I don't want to speak and I get up and try and push past her, but she grabs my arm.

'Eddie,' she says and she's got this really kind voice. 'Eddie, I'm so sorry. I'm so sorry.' And I look up at her then and she's looking at me with these tears in her eyes, like she really is sorry. And when I see that, I feel the tears coming in my own eyes, and I know the last thing I need is to start crying in school like a great wuss, so I shake her off, tell her I'm fine and leave her to it.

That night after tea I want to be on my own, but the minute I go and lie on my bed Sam comes in and starts talking to me, and when I go downstairs and sit on the sofa Lucy comes in and tries to sit on my knee. I move her off, go up into Granddad's room and shut the door.

I sit there for ages looking around and thinking it all over. Most of his stuff has been taken away but suddenly I spot his old tobacco tin on the shelf. I go over and pick it up. I breathe it in and it smells like him; I remember seeing it in his hands so many times, and before I can stop them the stupid tears are there again, but this time they're not sad tears, they are angry tears, because I'm totally, totally mad at him for going away and leaving me. I'm mad at everyone for letting it happen. My fingers clench around the tin and I feel myself getting madder and madder and then I chuck it as hard as I can against the wall. It smashes open and tobacco flies everywhere.

I hear voices downstairs and Sam bursts in.

'Eddie, Eddie - there's a girl here to see you,' he says, all exited, then, looking round, 'what happened to Granddad's tobacco?' I ignore him and stomp downstairs thinking it must be Rosie and I'll have to tell her to go away until - I can't believe it - I see Dionne standing in our hallway. She looks kind of nervous.

'You didn't look like you wanted to talk to anyone at school,' she says, 'so I thought I'd come and see you. I hope you don't mind. I'll understand if you want me to go.' But the last thing I want is for her to go; Lucy is pulling her by the hand, and Sam is staring at her like he's never seen a girl before and my mum's going,

'You must be Dionne. It's very nice of you to come. Let's go through and I'll get you a drink.' How does my mum know it's Dionne? She's never seen her in her life before. I follow them into the kitchen.

Half an hour later we've had a couple of cokes and some biscuits, Sam's shown Dionne loads of pictures of Granddad when he was young, and Dionne's told us all about her mum and sister going away to London and how she misses them and has to live with her gran who's always out dancing covered in sequins, or doing stuff at the church. Then Lucy says,

'Hey, Granddad used to like dancing - if he hadn't died he could have been your gran's boyfriend.' And suddenly we are all laughing; we laugh so much that we're even crying and I can't tell if I'm crying because I'm laughing or I'm crying because I'm sad, but somehow it doesn't matter.

Later when Dionne's gone and the kids are in bed, Mum says,

'She's a nice girl, Eddie, that Dionne.' I don't say anything but I look over at her. Her eyes are puffy and she looks kind of old. She looks sad.

'You alright, Mum?' I go. She nods.

'I'm alright, love, but sometimes it's hard putting on a

brave face. That's something your granddad was good at. I learned it off him.' She looks back at me.

'He thought the world of you, Eddie, your granddad did. He said you were brave.' I shake my head and feel the tears coming back as I think of all the nice stuff Granddad used to say to me, even when I didn't deserve it. Then I think back to the last thing he said to me. It was the day before he died, but of course I didn't know it then.

'You've got to keep your chin up, Eddie,' he said, in his rough voice, 'and help those little ones to remember the good times.' Then he gave me that look he always gave me, the look that made me feel kind of proud and ashamed at the same time.

'But I know you will, Eddie,' he said, 'because you're a good lad. You always have been. One of the best.'

Episode 13
Then and now

Part 1

ROSIE

    This has been the best year of my life and the worst year of my life. The worst bit was that time I asked Eddie out and he looked at me as if he'd rather go out with a hippo from the zoo and told me it was Dionne he liked. I thought I'd die of shame. How could I have got it so wrong? I'd thought he was being kind to me and telling me about his running because he really liked me, but now I know he just felt sorry for me. I have never felt so awful and ashamed and embarrassed in my entire life. I didn't know how I could even look at him ever again.

And that wasn't the worst of it. I'd got myself in such a state thinking Dionne must have known all along – I just kept thinking about the two of them laughing about me and it got worse and worse. I ended up texting her and telling her I hated her and she could have Eddie if she wanted him. So the next day she wasn't speaking to me and I wanted to die. The only good thing was Eddie not coming to school so at least I didn't have to face him.

Then that night Dionne texted me and told me Eddie's granddad had died and that's why he wasn't at school and she said she liked Eddie but didn't fancy him and she'd never wanted him to fancy her so why did I hate her? So I texted her and said I was sorry but she didn't text back so I still wanted to die.

Dionne didn't speak to me all that week and she didn't come to training, so Friday night I got up my courage and went round her house.

I told her I'd heard Letitia say she was considering her for the team and that I was worried that if she didn't train she'd lose her chance. And she said she didn't care if she got in the team or not and if I hated her so much why didn't I just leave her alone because with friends like me who needed enemies. But I kept on telling her I was so sorry about that text and that I'd only sent it because I'd felt such a fool about Eddie and everything.

Anyway she didn't seem so mad after that, and then we just started talking about Eddie and I told her all that fancying stuff had just been stupid; then we both said how sad it was about his granddad because he'd been like the best person in Eddie's life. And after that we got sort of OK again - but it was still the worst time of my whole life.

Best things have been winning that enterprise award, getting the teen café idea going, being girl of the match five times and my dad getting a job. It's back to normal now at home - we're even going to Disneyland next week and Dionne's coming with us. But I think best of all is that in spite of everything I sort of feel alright. Like I used to think I was just fat and thick and hopeless, but Miss Forest got us to do this thing in our tutor where each person in a group had to write one positive thing about the others and this is what the five people in my group wrote about me:

She never gives up.

She's honest and brave.

She makes things happen.

She always gives her best shot.

And my favourite one:

She's great to talk to because she always listens.

I felt so good when I read those things that, even though I know I got myself in a mess over Eddie and upset Dionne and behaved like a total idiot, now I tell myself I can get through stuff like that. I tell myself that everybody does stupid stuff sometimes.

I've got loads of friends, not just Dionne, but Maddie and Laura and some of the girls in year eight. So now if Katie or Suzy start bitching at me I just tell myself they're really sad people – I don't let them get to me. I feel OK enough now to just walk away.

Part 2

EDDIE

I thought I'd never get over Granddad dying and I still miss him, but sometimes it's almost like he's still there in my head, talking to me. Like when I started running he'd sit on our front step timing me with this enormous stop-watch to make sure I beat my previous time.

'Great,' he'd say if I did it faster, or, 'have a break and then do it again, lad,' if I didn't. Now it's Sam sitting there with the watch, but it's Granddad's voice that keeps me going. It was his voice I was listening to when I won the five hundred meters today for sports day with everyone standing there looking totally amazed.

'So where did that speed come from?' Rafiq asked me, 'you weren't exactly fit the last time we had to run anywhere.'

Rafiq and me are mostly OK now. He's changed a lot since that day he got mud on my trousers and maybe I've changed too. We don't ever hang around together but he's not so up himself and out on his own like he used to be. He's safe.

I still like Dionne and I still think she's fit but I know she'll never want to be more than a friend and I can live with that. I'm not that same saddo who used to hang around her all the time. I've got new mates now who I go round with and, to be honest, I'm so busy keeping the website up-to-date and running every night, I don't have time for much else.

That Karl has left the school and gone to live with his gran in Scotland because his dad got put in prison for beating up a taxi driver. Rafiq said it was a racist attack and good riddance to the scumbags – they'd got what they deserved, but I felt bad because I reckoned that if Karl's dad was violent and racist then so would Karl be I suppose. Like it doesn't make him right, but it makes you think why he might be like that. I did a blog entry on Rafiq's issues page about how some parents fill their kids with that sort of racist crap. I guess I was lucky having Granddad - and I know I'm lucky to have Mum.

Part 3

It's been quite a year, ups and downs. Best was playing in the team for the last match of the season and Chantelle coming down to watch and then telling me she's got herself a job down here and she's back for good. She says she'd rather be here with me with less money than go back to London. Yessss!

Bad thing - Mum's still there - but she might come back soon as well. I phoned her up and told her what I thought for once, instead of just pouring it all out in my diary.

'You're our mum and you should be here with us,' I said to her. 'What's the point of being a mother if you don't ever see us?' I didn't even shout. Chantelle says yelling gets you nowhere except in trouble and should be saved for emergencies. She's so cool.

Another bad thing was when Rosie sent me that text because of Eddie. It really upset me at the time but we got over it. In fact I'm going with her whole family to Disneyland next week, which is amazing. Chantelle's bought me some new T-shirts and these really cool trainers.

I think Miss Forest has made a difference to our tutor. She gets us to talk about stuff – like what bugs us and what's good – and girls like Laura and Rosie who used to be kind of quiet and shy aren't afraid anymore of saying things out loud. Even the boys are talking about stuff now instead of making stupid jokes and messing around all the time.

Laura and her mates have got into saving the world recently, and Laura stood up and sounded off about teachers who drive big cars to school.

'Don't they know they're destroying our planet?' she said. Miss Forest told her to write something on the website. Good job she cycles to school.

And then there was Eddie being so cut up about his granddad dying. That was bad. Rosie and I decided I should be the one to go round his house and try and cheer him up, so I did and it was nice. His little brother and sister are so cute. I think Eddie was glad I went, but I don't reckon he fancies me any more. At first I was glad he didn't, but today at sports day he won the five hundred meters – he was so fast I could hardly believe it - and all these girls were cheering – they actually seemed to think he was hot. I even found myself looking at him and thinking how much he'd changed and……well……hmm …?

Part 4

Well this year has been something else. I came top in every single test so no surprises there, but coming top doesn't really seem that great when I think about other stuff – like how bad it feels when you realise nobody likes you, and how good it is to have a few mates.

Before I started at this school I never knew I was lonely; I used to tell myself I was a loner because I wanted to be and everyone else was an idiot, but now I look at Prahlad and I think OK, so he works hard and he gets all these A stars, but he never has fun or does anything much and I know I don't want to be like that.

Not that it's easy or anything, getting friends – like I'd never want to be mates with Eddie and that lot any more than they'd want to be mates with me - but Li is OK, and this other kid Sean is alright too. It's good just having someone to hang around with sometimes.

The other good thing is my dad actually forgetting how mad he was at me for getting in that fight and starting to get involved in our racism blog. At first it was a nightmare

– he tried to get me to put all this boring stuff in about discrimination law and stuff. But when I told him it was a blog and not one of his lectures, and that he didn't have to tell me how I felt about racist stuff because I knew how I felt, he told me to go for it, and he told me he was proud of me.

He'd never said anything like that to me before. And now he even takes time to read the whole page every day, which is amazing like we're actually speaking to each other!

Yeh – when I think it over I reckon year eight will be different from year seven. I think it's going to be alright.